LOVE IN GREECE

TRUE LOVE

MOLLIE MATHEWS

Blue Orchid
PUBLISHING

TRUE LOVE

LOVE IN GREECE:
TRUE LOVE SERIES

MOLLIE MATHEWS

JOIN THE CLUB

Never miss a new release or giveaway! Sign up for Mollie's newsletter to stay in the loop—and receive a free love story. Check out a full list of books and bio at www.molliemathews.com. Follow Mollie on Social Media as @Molliewritesromance (because she does) And if you loved this book, please take a moment to leave a review once you're done. Thank you!

Follow my author page and never miss a new release!

AMAZON: Author.to/MollieMathews

BOOKBUB: https://www.bookbub.com/authors/mollie-mathews

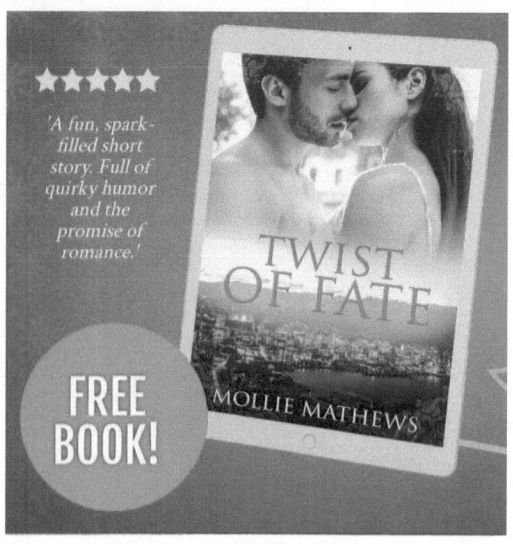

LOVE IN GREECE...

In the world of power and wealth, love is the last thing on their minds...

Billionaire Aris Kostas has always believed that marriage is a duty, not a matter of the heart. When he proposes to Sophia Leonides, it's a perfect business arrangement—an alliance to save her crumbling family and secure his reputation. He's made it clear: love has no place in their union.

But on the eve of their wedding, Aris reveals a devastating truth. He doesn't love her and never will. Heartbroken yet bound by obligation, Sophia walks down the aisle, prepared to live a life of cold formality. But as the days turn into weeks, an undeniable spark begins to flicker between them, challenging everything they thought they knew about marriage, loyalty, and love.

When a family scandal threatens to destroy everything Aris has built, Sophia steps up as his partner, forcing Aris to confront the walls he's built around his heart. Together, they face the pressures of high society, the ruthless world of business, and the undeniable pull between them.

Will their marriage of convenience remain a contract, or

will love find its way through the cracks of their carefully constructed lives?

Love in Greece is a captivating, emotionally charged romance that will sweep you off your feet. Perfect for fans of billionaire romances, slow-burn love stories, and high-stakes emotional drama, this novel will leave you breathless.

Grab your copy today and fall in love with Aris and Sophia's journey to true happiness!

PRAISE FOR THE TRUE LOVE SERIES

Psychology rules in this romance of personalities

"I enjoyed reading "Love in Sicily," not only because the setting is one of my favorite places in the world. And not only because I enjoy a good, quick romantic read. This book is even more than just a romance. The survival guilt of the main character starts the psychology going that pulls you into the character of Kate. Her emotions are in full force every step of the way and keep you reading. So it is no surprise that when she meets Gianni emotions run high. And then we even learn a bit about Gianni's issues. I'll stop here so there are no spoiler alerts, except to say I was happy with the ending. I appreciated the author's understanding of survivor guilt and have a feeling she did some research before writing the novel, which I really liked."

~ Amazon 5-Star Review

A warmly romantic story

"Love In Venice is a warmly romantic story. I loved that their hearts seemed to speak to each other almost from their first meeting. I love that we get to see how their lives unfold and their beautiful love for each other."

~ **JoAnne W.**

"*Love in Montana* will grab you and keep you intrigued throughout. Lizzie went through so much upheaval, it was amazing the adjustments she made to her life. She is so talented and beautiful inside and out. Jack would do anything for those he loves, I loved watching him meet the obstacles put in his way. I absolutely loved the awesome ending I'm so glad it went the way it did."

~ **Amazon 5-Star Review**

1

A PROPOSAL OF CONVENIENCE

Aris Kostas had always known his life would be dictated by duty, not desire. As a billionaire heir to one of the largest shipping empires in Greece, he never questioned the responsibilities that came with his name. And now, standing before the sprawling estate of the Leonides family, he was about to solidify that legacy with a marriage born out of necessity rather than love.

Sophia Leonides, the youngest daughter of a once-prominent aristocratic family, met his gaze with a steady calm that belied the desperation her family was facing. Their fortunes had crumbled over the years, and with no prospects in sight, their future rested on this union. Her father, once a man of influence, had arranged the meeting, hoping that Sophia's beauty and grace would be enough to lure a man like Aris into a proposal.

But Sophia had never imagined herself standing at the mercy of a man like Aris Kostas. Tall, brooding, and with a reputation for being as cold as the marble halls of his family's estate, he was not the prince charming of her childhood fantasies. Yet here she was, agreeing to a marriage that had little to do with her own desires.

"I believe we understand each other," Aris said, his voice as smooth and measured as ever. "This is not a love match, but a partnership. Your family will be cared for, and in return, you will uphold the dignity of being Mrs. Kostas."

Sophia nodded, feeling the weight of her decision settle like a stone in her chest. Her heart ached for a different future, but reality had made the decision for her. There was no turning back now. "I understand," she replied softly.

Aris's dark eyes searched hers for a moment, perhaps seeking any sign of hesitation, but when he found none, he extended a hand. "Then we are agreed. We'll announce the engagement tomorrow."

Sophia took his hand, feeling the coolness of his skin against hers. It was done. In a few months, she would be Mrs. Aris Kostas, a title that held more prestige than warmth. As they sealed the agreement, Sophia couldn't help but wonder if this decision would be the one that saved her or condemned her to a life as cold as Aris's gaze.

She glanced up at him one last time, hoping to see something—anything—that would give her reassurance. But Aris had already turned away, his mind on the empire he was building, not on the woman he was about to marry.

2

THE GLAMOUR OF HIGH SOCIETY

The engagement of Aris Kostas and Sophia Leonides was the talk of Greece. It was plastered across every newspaper, the photographs of them together carefully curated to project an image of power and elegance. Aris, with his chiseled jaw and composed demeanor, looked every bit the billionaire magnate, while Sophia, in her designer dresses and poised expressions, played her role to perfection. But behind the glamour, a different reality brewed —one Sophia couldn't quite escape.

As she adjusted the diamond earrings Aris had given her, Sophia looked into the mirror and barely recognized the woman staring back. Her hair was swept into an elegant chignon, and her makeup was flawless, but there was an emptiness in her eyes that no amount of beauty could mask. Tonight, like every night since their engagement, they would attend another high-society event, another glittering gala where their engagement would be paraded for all to see.

Sophia smoothed the front of her evening gown and sighed. The Kostas family had made it clear what they expected from her: grace, dignity, and absolute loyalty to the family's image. But that image felt like a prison. Every dinner, every charity function, and every public appearance reinforced the fact that her role was more ornamental than emotional. Her life had become a series of posed smiles and carefully rehearsed conversations, each word measured to protect the Kostas name.

As she descended the grand staircase of Aris' estate, her eyes caught sight of him waiting at the bottom. Dressed impeccably in a tailored suit, he was the epitome of control. He looked up as she approached, his expression unreadable. There was no warmth, no admiration in his gaze—just a businesslike acknowledgment that she had fulfilled her part of the bargain by looking the part of his future wife.

"You look beautiful," Aris said, his voice as even as ever. There was no passion behind the words, but Sophia had grown accustomed to the formality of their interactions.

"Thank you," she replied, offering a smile that didn't reach her eyes.

The car ride to the gala was quiet, the only sound being the hum of the engine as the city of Athens flashed by. As they pulled up to the event, the paparazzi swarmed the entrance, their cameras flashing like fireworks. Aris stepped out first, offering his hand to Sophia. She took it, and for a moment, she felt the strange, cold comfort of his touch. It wasn't love, but it was something steady. Predictable.

Inside, the event was a sea of glittering chandeliers and designer gowns. Every major player in Greek high society was there, from business tycoons to politicians. Sophia felt the eyes of the room fall upon her and Aris as they entered, whispers trailing in their wake.

"She's beautiful, isn't she?" one woman whispered, her voice barely audible.

"Yes, but I wonder if there's anything between them," another replied. "He always looks so... detached."

Sophia pretended not to hear, though the words struck her deeper than she expected. She was becoming accustomed to the role of the perfect fiancée, but the reality of it all was beginning to suffocate her.

As the night wore on, Aris mingled effortlessly with the guests, discussing business ventures and future investments. Sophia stood by his side, nodding when appropriate, offering polite smiles to the elite crowd. Yet, even as she played her part flawlessly, she felt an overwhelming sense of isolation. Aris moved through the room as if he were born to it, his every word calculated and precise. She, on the other hand, felt like an outsider looking in.

At one point in the evening, Aris' mother, Eleni Kostas, approached them. She was a statuesque woman with an air of command that was impossible to ignore. "Sophia," she greeted her with a tight smile, "I see you're adjusting well to your new role."

"I'm doing my best," Sophia replied, her voice as measured as she could manage.

Eleni's eyes flickered with approval but quickly moved on to Aris. "We must ensure everything is perfect for the wedding," she said, her tone sharp. "The Kostas name demands it."

Aris gave a curt nod, his expression as unreadable as ever. "Everything will be as it should," he assured his mother.

Sophia stood there, feeling like a prop in their conversation. She knew that to Eleni, the wedding was not about love or happiness but about maintaining the family's pristine image. Her role was clear: she was to be the beautiful, obedient wife who would secure Aris' place in society. Love, passion, and personal fulfillment were luxuries she wasn't afforded.

As the night came to a close, Sophia found herself standing alone on a balcony overlooking the city. The twinkling lights of Athens stretched out before her, and for a moment, she allowed herself to breathe. The mask she wore for the world slipped away, if only briefly, and she wondered how long she could continue like this. How long could she live a life of empty promises and shallow smiles?

Aris appeared beside her, his presence quiet but commanding. "It was a successful evening," he said, his voice as cool as the night air.

"Yes," Sophia replied, though her heart wasn't in it.

For a moment, they stood in silence, the weight of unspoken words hanging between them. Sophia turned to look at him, searching his face for any sign of emotion, but as always, there was none. He was a man made of marble, unyielding and perfect on the outside, but hollow within.

"Is this what you want, Aris?" she asked softly, surprising even herself with the question.

He didn't look at her, his gaze fixed on the city below. "It doesn't matter what I want," he said, his voice low. "This is what needs to be done."

Sophia felt a pang of sadness at his words. She realized then that they were both trapped—Aris by his duty to his family, and she by her need to save hers. Neither had chosen this path, yet both were walking it.

As they returned to the party, hand in hand for the world to see, Sophia couldn't help but wonder if this was the life she was meant to live—or if she would one day find the courage to break free.

3

BEHIND CLOSED DOORS

From the outside, Aris Kostas seemed every bit the perfect heir—impeccably groomed, composed, and unwavering. He conducted business with precision, made decisions with calculated foresight, and charmed high society without ever allowing them a glimpse beneath the surface. But behind the doors of his penthouse, away from the public eye, Aris was a man at war with himself.

He sat in his study, the late-night silence heavy around him. The engagement had gone off without a hitch, the wedding preparations were underway, and Sophia had played her role with the grace expected of her. Yet, something gnawed at him, an unfamiliar sensation that he couldn't quite shake. It wasn't love—he'd long since abandoned any belief in such a frivolous notion—but it was something. A pull, a curiosity, a desire to understand this woman who had become part of his life in such a short time.

Sophia.

He thought of her now, likely sleeping in her own bed in her family's estate, far from his world of endless responsibilities. She was an enigma to him. Quiet, composed, and always polite, she fulfilled every expectation he'd had of her as a fiancée. But in those fleeting moments when her guard slipped, he saw something more. A flicker of vulnerability in her eyes, a trace of longing in her soft words. She was playing the part, just as he was, but he sensed that it came at a greater cost to her.

Aris leaned back in his chair, staring at the fireplace as the flames flickered and danced. He had never been one to indulge in emotions. From a young age, he had been groomed for one purpose: to uphold the Kostas name, to lead the empire his father had built, and to continue the legacy. There had been no room for softness, no space for vulnerability. His father had drilled it into him time and again—emotion was weakness, and weakness had no place in the world of power.

But lately, Sophia's presence was beginning to chip away at the walls he had built around himself. He could see her struggle, though she hid it well. The loneliness, the isolation she must feel as she navigated this new world of wealth and power. She had agreed to this marriage out of necessity, just as he had. Yet, unlike him, she hadn't known a life of duty and obligation. She had been thrust into it, and Aris couldn't help but wonder if she regretted her decision.

With a sigh, Aris stood and poured himself a glass of whiskey, the amber liquid swirling in the glass as he stared out over the city. Athens glittered beneath him, the city that his family had helped shape and control for generations. This was his world—one of power, wealth, and endless expectation. He had always accepted that this was his path, but now, with Sophia in the picture, he found himself questioning things he had never questioned before.

Was this all there was? A life of calculated moves and cold transactions? Could there be something more, something deeper, waiting for him if he allowed it?

He took a sip of his whiskey, the burn of the alcohol doing little to dull the thoughts racing through his mind. He had chosen Sophia because she fit the mold—beautiful, poised, and from a family that, while fallen from grace, still carried a respectable name. But there was more to her than that. He could see it in the way she held herself, the quiet strength she carried, even as she was thrust into a life she hadn't chosen. And though he had told himself he didn't care about her feelings, he couldn't deny that her quiet sadness affected him in ways he didn't expect.

The memory of her eyes from the night before lingered in his mind. She had looked at him with such vulnerability when he told her he didn't love her. Aris had thought he was doing the right thing, sparing her any illusions, but now he wondered if he had only hurt her. He had seen the disappointment flash across her face, though she had quickly masked it with a polite nod. She was good at that— hiding her emotions, just as he was. But there had been something raw in that moment, something that had made him feel like he had let her down in a way he didn't fully understand.

He drained the last of his whiskey and set the glass down with a thud. Aris was not a man who second-guessed his decisions, but now, in the quiet of his study, he found himself questioning everything. His father had taught him that love was unnecessary, a distraction from the real goals of life— power, wealth, and control. But as he thought of Sophia, he couldn't help but wonder if perhaps his father had been wrong.

Across town, Sophia lay awake in her bed, staring at the ceiling. The room was quiet, save for the soft ticking of the clock on the nightstand. Her engagement ring, heavy on her finger, glittered in the moonlight that filtered through the window. She turned the ring absentmindedly, feeling its weight, both literal and metaphorical.

She had known what she was getting into with Aris. Their engagement had been one of necessity, not love, and she had accepted that. But she hadn't anticipated the loneliness that would come with it—the hollow feeling that settled in her chest every time she saw Aris and realized that he viewed her not as a partner, but as a means to an end.

And yet, there was something about him that intrigued her. He was distant, cold even, but in those rare moments when his guard slipped, she glimpsed something deeper. A flicker of vulnerability, of a man who was just as trapped by his circumstances as she was. She wanted to understand him, to know the man behind the billionaire facade, but every time she tried to reach him, he withdrew further.

Sophia sighed, turning on her side and pulling the covers up around her. She had agreed to this marriage to save her family, but now she couldn't help but wonder if she had condemned herself to a life of emptiness. Aris was a man she could admire, even respect, but could she ever love him? And more importantly, could he ever love her?

As the city slept around them, both Aris and Sophia lay awake, each wrestling with their own thoughts, their own doubts. They were two people bound together by circumstance, but separated by walls of their own making. Neither knew what the future held, but one thing was certain: the path ahead would not be easy.

4

THE NIGHT BEFORE

The night before the wedding arrived with a heaviness that neither Aris nor Sophia had anticipated. The Kostas estate was aglow with preparations, the staff bustling to ensure every detail of the grand affair was in place. Sophia sat in her private suite, her wedding gown hanging on the door—a masterpiece of silk and lace, chosen not by her but by Aris' mother. It was perfect, just like everything else in this marriage was supposed to be.

But her heart wasn't in it.

The weight of tomorrow pressed down on her, and despite the opulence surrounding her, Sophia felt more trapped than ever. She thought about her family—how much they needed this, how her father had all but begged her to go through with the engagement. For them, this marriage was salvation. For her, it was starting to feel like a prison.

A knock at the door broke her thoughts. Sophia opened it to find Aris standing there, his expression unreadable, but there was something in his eyes—something she couldn't quite place.

"Can I come in?" he asked, his voice low.

She stepped aside, letting him enter the room. He moved with the same quiet confidence that always surrounded him, but tonight there was a tension between them that had been growing steadily since their engagement.

Aris stood in the center of the room, his hands in his pockets, as if struggling with what to say. Sophia watched him, waiting. He had never come to her like this before—not in private, not with an air of vulnerability. She had always seen him as a man of stone, unyielding, and distant. Tonight, he seemed different.

"I wanted to talk to you before the wedding," Aris began, his eyes meeting hers briefly before flickering away. "There's something you need to know."

Sophia's heart skipped a beat, anxiety tightening in her chest. She wasn't sure what she had expected from this conversation, but there was something about Aris' tone that made her feel uneasy.

He took a breath, and for the first time since she had met him, he looked... uncertain. "I need to be honest with you, Sophia," he said quietly. "Tomorrow, we will stand before everyone and vow to spend our lives together. But I can't stand up there with you under false pretenses."

She frowned, confused. "What do you mean?"

Aris hesitated, running a hand through his hair—an action that, to her surprise, made him look almost human. "I don't love you," he said bluntly, the words hanging in the air between them like a weight. "I never will."

The impact of his confession hit her like a punch to the stomach. Sophia's breath caught in her throat, her mind racing to process what he had just said. It wasn't that she hadn't known their marriage was one of convenience, but hearing the words spoken so plainly, so coldly, made it all too real.

Aris watched her reaction closely, his expression tight. "I thought it was better to tell you now than to let you believe that anything would change after tomorrow. I've always been clear about my intentions, and I won't lie to you about this."

Sophia stood frozen, her mind spinning. She had known this was not a love match, but a part of her—small, naive—had hoped that maybe, with time, things would grow between them. That maybe, after the wedding, they could build something real, something more than just a cold arrangement.

But now, those hopes were shattered.

"Why are you telling me this now?" she asked, her voice barely above a whisper.

Aris sighed, stepping closer to her, his expression softened but still guarded. "Because it wouldn't be fair to let you believe there's something more. I don't want to lie to you, Sophia. I respect you too much for that."

Respect. The word felt hollow, empty in the context of everything she was feeling. Sophia turned away from him, her hands trembling as she tried to hold herself together. She had agreed to this marriage to save her family, but the reality of what that truly meant was now staring her in the face. This wasn't just a loveless marriage—it was a marriage where love wasn't even possible.

She felt the tears prick at her eyes but refused to let them fall. Crying now wouldn't help. It wouldn't change anything. Still, the pain of hearing him say those words, the finality of it, broke something inside her.

"I see," she managed to say, her voice tight with the effort of holding back her emotions. "Thank you for your honesty."

Aris watched her carefully, his expression unreadable

again. "You can walk away," he said after a moment. "If you want to. I won't stop you."

Sophia's heart raced. Walk away? Could she even do that? The idea of walking out on this wedding—on everything that had been planned, on everything her family had staked their future on—seemed impossible. But the alternative was just as terrifying: a life bound to a man who had just told her he would never love her.

"I can't," she whispered, more to herself than to him. She couldn't leave, not when her family was depending on her. Not when so many eyes were on them, waiting for this wedding to cement their place in society. She had made a choice, and now she had to live with it.

Aris nodded, his jaw tight, as if he had expected that answer all along. "I understand," he said quietly.

For a long moment, they stood in silence, the air between them thick with unsaid words. Sophia stared at the floor, trying to reconcile the conflicting emotions swirling inside her. She wanted to hate him for his coldness, for his detachment, but she couldn't. Because deep down, she knew that he was being honest in a way that no one else in her life had been.

Finally, Aris turned to leave, but just before he reached the door, he paused, looking back at her. "You deserve better," he said softly, almost as if the words were meant for himself as much as for her. And then, without another word, he left, the door closing behind him with a soft click.

Sophia stood alone in the room, the silence overwhelming. She stared at her wedding dress, hanging so innocently on the door, and felt a surge of anger and sadness rise within her. This was supposed to be her future, the path she had chosen. But now, she wasn't sure if it was a path she could walk without losing herself.

As the night wore on, Sophia found herself wondering what tomorrow would bring. She would marry Aris Kostas, the billionaire who didn't love her, and she would play her role in the grand spectacle of their lives. But at what cost? And could she bear the weight of it?

5

AN UNEXPECTED REVELATION

The morning light streamed through the grand windows of the Kostas estate, casting long shadows on the polished marble floors. Sophia hadn't slept a wink. The events of the previous night played over and over in her mind, leaving her torn between duty and her crumbling hope for something more. Today was her wedding day—a day that was supposed to mark the beginning of a new life, yet it felt like the end of something precious she hadn't even known she wanted.

The household bustled with activity as the final preparations for the wedding were underway. Sophia, still dressed in her robe, sat in front of the mirror, watching the makeup artist work on her pale face. She barely recognized the reflection staring back at her—a woman preparing to marry a man who had just confessed he would never love her.

Her best friend, Elena, arrived quietly, slipping into the room with a grace that only she could manage in such an overwhelming situation. Elena had always been a grounding presence in Sophia's life, the one person who could make sense of chaos. Today, however, even Elena seemed unsure of how to offer comfort.

"Sophia," Elena said softly, dismissing the makeup artist with a gentle wave. "Are you alright? You look like you haven't slept."

Sophia blinked, her hands resting listlessly in her lap. "I haven't," she admitted, her voice sounding distant to her own ears. "Aris... He came to me last night."

Elena's eyes widened slightly, her concern deepening. "What happened? Did he say something?"

Sophia took a deep breath, trying to steady her trembling hands. "He told me he doesn't love me, and he never will. He said it wasn't fair to let me believe otherwise."

The weight of the confession hung in the air between them, and Elena's face softened with sympathy. "Oh, Sophia..."

"I don't know what to do," Sophia whispered, the words laced with the ache of uncertainty. "He said I could walk away, but how can I? My family... they need this. I agreed to this marriage, knowing it wasn't about love, but now..." Her voice faltered, her heart heavy with the knowledge that her hopes for something more had been crushed.

Elena knelt in front of her, taking Sophia's cold hands in her own. "You don't have to go through with this. You're allowed to change your mind. You're allowed to want more than just an arrangement."

Sophia shook her head, feeling the sting of tears she refused to let fall. "I can't. If I leave, my family will lose everything. I'd be shamed, and my father... I don't even know how we'd survive. I don't have a choice."

Elena's brow furrowed in frustration. "But you do have a choice, Sophia. You've always had a choice. This is your life.

You shouldn't have to sacrifice your happiness for anyone else's sake."

"I don't know if I even know what happiness is anymore," Sophia said bitterly. "I made this deal to save my family. I thought I could live with that, but now…"

A long silence stretched between them, broken only by the distant sounds of wedding preparations echoing through the halls. Finally, Elena spoke again, her voice gentle but firm. "Then maybe the real question is: Can you live with him? Can you live in a marriage where there's no hope for love?"

Sophia looked at her friend, the reality of Elena's question sinking in. Could she live in a world where she was bound to a man who saw her as nothing more than a part of his empire? A marriage of duty, without love, without affection? She had once thought she could, but now, after Aris' confession, she wasn't so sure.

As if summoned by the weight of her thoughts, a knock came at the door. Sophia's heart skipped a beat, wondering if it was Aris again. But when the door opened, it was Nikos, Aris' younger brother, stepping inside. Unlike Aris, Nikos carried a warmth that immediately eased the tension in the room. His disheveled hair and slightly rumpled suit made him seem more approachable, less imposing.

"Sophia," Nikos greeted her with a gentle smile, but there was a seriousness in his eyes. "Could I have a word?"

Elena squeezed Sophia's hands one last time before standing and excusing herself, leaving them alone.

Nikos crossed the room and sat down across from her, his gaze soft but concerned. "I'm not going to pretend to know what's going through Aris' head," he began, "but I need you to know something. You deserve more than what he's giving you."

Sophia raised her eyes to meet his, surprised by the directness of his words. "You're his brother. Why would you say that?"

Nikos leaned forward slightly, his voice low but earnest. "Because I care about both of you. And because I've seen Aris bury his emotions so deep, even he's convinced himself that they don't exist. He's lived his whole life thinking he doesn't need love, that duty is all that matters. But I've seen the way he looks at you, Sophia. He might not say it, he might not even admit it to himself, but he feels something for you. I know it."

Sophia stared at him, her heart pounding. "But he told me last night... he said he could never love me."

Nikos sighed, rubbing a hand over his face. "That's Aris being Aris. He's always been scared of vulnerability, scared of letting anyone close enough to hurt him. But I've seen it. He's changing, even if he won't admit it."

Sophia shook her head, confusion clouding her mind. "I don't know if I can live in a marriage where I'm constantly wondering if he'll ever care for me the way I care for him."

Nikos paused for a moment, considering her words carefully. "You have to decide what's best for you, Sophia. But just know that Aris isn't as heartless as he makes himself out to be. He's human, just like the rest of us. And sometimes, the people who seem the coldest are the ones who need love the most."

Sophia looked down at her hands, the weight of Nikos' words pressing heavily on her heart. Could it be true? Could Aris, the man who had spent their entire engagement keeping her at arm's length, actually care for her in some way? And if so, was that enough to give her hope for a future together?

Nikos stood up, offering her a small smile. "Whatever

you decide, I'll support you. But if you ever need someone to talk to, I'm here."

As he left, Sophia was left alone with her thoughts once again. The revelation that Aris might feel something for her, even if he couldn't admit it, both comforted and confused her. But it didn't change the fact that she was about to marry a man who had told her he would never love her.

The clock ticked on, and soon, it would be time to make her way down the aisle. But the question still remained: Could she live with a marriage built on nothing but duty? Or was there a chance, no matter how small, that love could grow from the ruins of their arrangement?

6

WALKING DOWN THE AISLE

The grand cathedral stood towering and majestic, adorned with white roses and gold accents, a testament to the opulence of the Kostas family. It was the wedding of the year, and everyone who mattered in Greece was in attendance. Sophia stood at the entrance, hidden from the crowd, the veil covering her face as she clutched her bouquet of roses so tightly her knuckles turned white.

The weight of the moment pressed heavily on her chest, making it hard to breathe. The organ music swelled through the grand hall, echoing off the vaulted ceilings as guests murmured in excitement. For them, this was a spectacle—an event filled with beauty and grandeur, a marriage of power and prestige. But for Sophia, it was something far more personal, far more uncertain.

She could hear the faint sounds of cameras clicking outside, the press eager to capture every moment of the Kostas wedding. But none of that mattered to her now. All she could think about was what lay ahead—walking down that long aisle toward a man who had confessed he would never love her.

As the music shifted, signaling her entrance, Sophia's heart began to race. Her father, beaming with pride, stepped beside her, offering his arm. He was dressed in his finest suit, his posture straighter than she had seen in years. For him, this wedding meant redemption. It was the lifeline that would save the Leonides family from financial ruin, and Sophia could see the relief in his eyes.

"You look beautiful, my dear," her father said softly, his voice filled with emotion. "This is a great day for us."

Sophia nodded, forcing a small smile. She knew what this day meant to her family, but inside, her heart felt heavy, torn between duty and the desire for something more. Her mind raced with the memory of Aris' confession, and Nikos' words that morning, still lingering in her thoughts. Could there be hope? Could Aris change, even if he didn't believe in love?

The doors to the cathedral opened, and the crowd turned to watch as she began her slow, measured walk down the aisle. The sunlight filtered through the stained glass windows, casting colorful beams across the marble floors. The air was filled with anticipation, the weight of hundreds of eyes on her as she made her way toward Aris.

She lifted her eyes, and there he was—Aris Kostas, standing at the altar, tall and composed, the picture of confidence. He was dressed in a perfectly tailored tuxedo, his expression as stoic as ever. But as she drew closer, Sophia thought she saw something flicker in his eyes—something that gave her pause. Was it regret? Doubt? Or perhaps something more?

Her father released her arm when they reached the altar, and for a moment, Sophia stood frozen, her breath catching in her throat. Aris turned to face her, his dark eyes locking onto hers, and in that brief exchange, the rest of the world seemed to fall away. There was something different in his gaze today. The cold detachment she had come to expect wasn't there. Instead, there was a tension, an uncertainty that she hadn't seen before.

The priest began speaking, his voice deep and reverent as he led them through the sacred vows. Sophia's hands trembled slightly as she held her bouquet, her mind a whirlwind of emotions. This was it. The moment when she would become Mrs. Aris Kostas, a title that held power but no promise of love.

When the priest asked if she would take Aris as her husband, her heart pounded in her chest. She could feel everyone's eyes on her, waiting for her to speak. She opened her mouth, but the words caught in her throat.

Aris leaned slightly toward her, his voice low, meant only for her. "Sophia," he whispered, his tone softer than she had ever heard before. "You don't have to do this if you don't want to. You can still walk away."

Her eyes flicked to his, searching for meaning behind his words. Did he truly mean it? Did he want her to walk away? Or was this his final attempt to give her a choice, to set her free from a life that might never bring her happiness?

"I can't," she whispered back, her voice trembling. "My family… I can't."

Aris' jaw tightened, and for a fleeting moment, she thought she saw a flash of something in his eyes—something like guilt or perhaps sorrow. He didn't want this either, she realized. Not in the way it had unfolded. And yet, here they were, bound by the expectations of everyone around them.

The priest continued, oblivious to the silent exchange between them, and soon it was Aris' turn to speak his vows. He cleared his throat, his voice steady and composed. "I,

Aris, take you, Sophia, to be my wife," he said, his words formal and rehearsed, but his gaze never left hers. "To have and to hold, from this day forward, for better or for worse."

Sophia's heart squeezed at the last words. For worse, she thought. That seemed far more likely than for better. And yet, as she looked into his eyes, she felt the tiniest glimmer of something shift between them. It wasn't love—not yet. But there was something there. A crack in the wall Aris had built around himself, something she hadn't expected to see.

When it was her turn to repeat her vows, she took a deep breath, her voice steady despite the whirlwind of emotions swirling inside her. "I, Sophia, take you, Aris, to be my husband," she said softly, her eyes locked on his. "To have and to hold, from this day forward, for better or for worse."

The words felt heavy with meaning, as if they were binding her not just to him, but to a life she wasn't sure she was ready for. But as she finished her vows, something unexpected happened. Aris' hand, which had been resting at his side, reached out, ever so slightly, to touch hers. His fingers brushed against hers, the contact brief but filled with an unspoken message.

It was as if he was telling her that, despite everything, he was here. That he wasn't as indifferent as he had made himself out to be. Sophia felt her breath catch at the touch, and in that moment, she realized something: she wasn't as alone in this as she had thought.

The ceremony continued, and when the priest declared them husband and wife, the crowd erupted in applause. Sophia and Aris turned to face their guests, a picture-perfect couple in the eyes of the world. But as they walked down the aisle together, side by side, Sophia couldn't shake the feeling that something had shifted between them—something small, but undeniable.

As they exited the cathedral, the sunlight blinding them for a moment, Aris leaned in, his voice low and close to her ear. "I don't know what the future holds," he murmured, his words filled with a quiet intensity. "But I'll try, Sophia. I'll try."

Her heart leapt at the unexpected promise. It wasn't love. It wasn't everything she had hoped for. But it was something. And for now, that was enough.

7

THE HONEYMOON DILEMMA

The honeymoon was supposed to be a dream, a time for newlyweds to revel in their love, but for Aris and Sophia, it was far from that. They had flown by private jet to Santorini, the jewel of the Aegean Sea, where white-washed villas clung to cliffs overlooking the sapphire waters. The setting was picturesque, the kind of place where romance should bloom effortlessly. Yet, the tension between them was palpable.

The first evening, they barely spoke. Aris had arranged for the most luxurious suite on the island, complete with a private infinity pool that seemed to melt into the horizon. The beauty of it was undeniable, but Sophia found little comfort in it. She stood on the terrace, watching the sunset paint the sky in shades of gold and pink, her thoughts far away from the serenity of their surroundings.

Aris, ever the enigma, sat inside, reviewing business emails on his phone. His silence gnawed at her, and though she hadn't expected a honeymoon filled with passion, the stark emotional distance between them felt unbearable. Sophia wrapped her arms around herself, trying to find solace in the beauty of Santorini, but her heart ached with uncertainty. She wanted to be anywhere but here—with him, in this emotional limbo.

Later that night, they sat at a private dinner on the cliffs. The table was set for two, candles flickering in the breeze, and the sound of the waves crashing below filled the silence between them. Sophia toyed with her fork, pushing the food around her plate, the weight of the unspoken tension thick in the air.

Aris watched her for a long moment before he finally spoke. "You've barely touched your food," he said, his voice quiet but firm. "If there's something bothering you, you should tell me."

Sophia put down her fork, her stomach churning with frustration. "What's bothering me?" she echoed, her voice tinged with disbelief. She met his gaze, her heart pounding. "What do you think is bothering me, Aris? We're on our honeymoon, and we're acting like strangers. I don't know how to talk to you. I don't even know if you want me here."

His jaw tightened, and for a moment, she thought he might snap back with one of his cold, calculated responses. But then, his gaze softened slightly, and he leaned back in his chair, exhaling deeply.

"Sophia, this… this wasn't how I expected things to go either," he admitted, surprising her. "I'm not good at this. I've never had to navigate a relationship like this before."

She scoffed, though the edge in her voice was less sharp than she intended. "Is that what this is? A relationship? Because it feels more like a business transaction."

Aris's eyes flashed with something—anger, perhaps, or frustration—but he didn't lash out. Instead, he ran a hand through his hair, his usually perfect composure unraveling just slightly. "I know that's how it must seem," he said, his voice low. "And I've done nothing to change that. But I'm trying."

Sophia's chest tightened at his words. She had heard him say he would try before, at the altar, but hearing it again, here, in the midst of their cold, uncomfortable honeymoon, made it feel less like a promise and more like a burden. Still, it was something—more than he had offered her before.

"Trying isn't enough, Aris," she said softly, her voice trembling. "I can't live in a marriage where we're constantly pretending. Where you keep me at arm's length, as if I'm just another piece in your life to manage."

He stared at her, the flickering candlelight casting shadows across his face. For a moment, he said nothing, and the silence between them grew heavy once more. Then, after what felt like an eternity, he spoke again, his voice barely above a whisper. "I don't know how to let you in."

The vulnerability in his voice caught her off guard. It was the first time he had admitted his struggle in such a raw, honest way. Sophia felt her anger fade, replaced by a deep sadness that they had reached this point. They were supposed to be partners, and yet they were both so far from what that meant.

"You don't have to be perfect, Aris," she said, her voice gentle. "I don't expect you to have all the answers. But I need to feel like you're in this with me. That we're not just two people sharing a life because we're obligated to."

Aris looked at her for a long moment, his expression unreadable. Then he nodded slowly, as if finally under-standing what she had been trying to tell him all along. "You're right," he said quietly. "I've been holding back because I don't know any other way. But I'm willing to try, Sophia. Really try."

His words, though hesitant, felt sincere, and for the first

time since their wedding, Sophia felt a flicker of hope. It wasn't much, but it was a start. She nodded, her heart still heavy but no longer weighed down by the hopelessness she had felt earlier.

"I don't need grand gestures, Aris," she said, her voice soft. "I just need you to be honest with me. To let me see who you really are."

Aris's gaze flickered with something—perhaps regret, perhaps relief—and he nodded again. "I'll try," he repeated, his voice firmer this time. "But it's not going to be easy."

Sophia gave him a small, tentative smile. "Nothing worth having ever is."

The dinner continued in silence, but the tension between them had shifted. It wasn't gone, but there was a new understanding, a fragile thread of connection that hadn't been there before. It wasn't love—not yet—but it was a beginning.

That night, as they returned to their villa, Sophia still slept in her own room, separate from Aris. But as she lay in bed, staring up at the ceiling, she no longer felt the crushing weight of isolation. Instead, there was a quiet, tentative hope that maybe—just maybe—things could change.

For the first time in days, Sophia drifted off to sleep with the faintest glimmer of possibility. She didn't know what the future held, but for now, she was willing to see where it might lead.

And as for Aris, lying alone in the room next door, he stared into the darkness, wrestling with emotions he had spent a lifetime trying to suppress. He didn't know how to love, not the way Sophia needed him to. But for her, he would try. And maybe—just maybe—that would be enough.

8

CRACKS IN THE ARMOR

The days on Santorini passed slowly, with Sophia and Aris caught in a strange limbo between distance and connection. They fell into a pattern of polite conversation during the day—exploring the island, dining in private, and attending a few social events with the other elite guests staying nearby. But at night, they continued to sleep in separate rooms, the invisible wall between them still standing, though now slightly cracked.

One evening, as the golden hour bathed the island in a warm, orange glow, Aris suggested a private dinner by the cliffs. The view was breathtaking, with the sun sinking into the sea, casting a shimmering path of light across the waves. It was the kind of place where dreams were born, but as they sat in silence, the weight of everything unspoken between them pressed heavily.

Sophia pushed her food around her plate, her appetite nonexistent. She had tried to be patient, to give Aris the space to work through whatever held him back, but the silence was suffocating her. Every small gesture he made—holding doors open, asking about her day—felt like a half-hearted attempt to keep up appearances. It was as if he didn't know how to bridge the gap between them, or worse, didn't truly want to.

Aris seemed tense, his gaze fixed on the horizon. His usual composed exterior was starting to show signs of strain, and Sophia could sense it. There was something simmering beneath the surface, something he wasn't saying.

Finally, she couldn't take it anymore. "Aris," she said, her voice soft but firm, "we can't keep pretending everything is fine. This... this distance between us is unbearable."

He blinked, clearly startled by her directness, but his expression remained neutral. "I'm not pretending," he said carefully, though his voice lacked conviction.

Sophia set her fork down and looked him in the eye. "You might not be, but I am. I'm pretending that I'm okay with this, with us living like strangers. But I'm not. I don't want to be in a marriage where we just... coexist."

Aris shifted in his chair, his face tightening. "I told you from the beginning what this would be," he said, his voice colder than she had expected. "I was clear."

"Yes, you were," she said, her frustration rising. "But people change, Aris. And I know you're not as indifferent as you pretend to be."

His eyes narrowed, a flicker of emotion crossing his face, but it was gone as quickly as it appeared. "You think you know me that well?"

Sophia leaned forward, her heart pounding. "I don't know you at all, because you won't let me. You've built this wall around yourself, and I've been trying to break through it. But you won't let me in. Why, Aris? Why won't you let me in?"

For a long moment, Aris said nothing. He stared at her, his jaw clenched, his eyes dark with something she couldn't quite place—fear, perhaps, or pain. Then, in a voice barely above a whisper, he said, "Because I don't know how."

The admission hung in the air, stark and raw. Sophia felt her breath catch in her throat, her heart aching at the vulnerability behind his words. Aris, the man who was always so controlled, so sure of himself, was admitting that he didn't know how to be open, how to let someone truly see him.

"I've never been close to anyone," he continued, his voice low, almost defeated. "Not like this. I was raised to focus on the business, on duty. Love wasn't something I was taught. It wasn't something I ever thought I needed."

Sophia's chest tightened. "But you do need it, Aris. We all do. You can't live your life shutting everyone out."

He looked away, his hands tightening into fists on the table. "You think I don't know that? You think I don't see what it's doing to us?" His voice grew harsher, frustration spilling over. "I don't want to hurt you, Sophia. But I don't know how to be what you need."

The honesty in his words broke something inside her, and suddenly, the anger she had been holding onto melted away. She could see the fear in him—the fear of vulnerability, of failure. He wasn't the cold, unfeeling man she had thought. He was a man who had spent his entire life building walls to protect himself, and now those walls were crumbling.

Sophia reached out, placing her hand over his, feeling the tension in his grip. "You don't have to be perfect, Aris," she said softly. "I don't need you to know everything, or have all the answers. I just need you to try."

He glanced down at her hand on his, his expression conflicted. For a long moment, he didn't move, as if unsure how to respond. Then, slowly, he relaxed his grip, his hand turning over to take hers.

"I'm scared," he admitted quietly, his eyes meeting hers at last. "I've never felt like this before. I don't know what to do with it."

Sophia's heart swelled at his words, the crack in his armor widening. She squeezed his hand gently, offering him a small, reassuring smile. "You don't have to do it alone. We'll figure it out together."

Aris looked at her, his gaze searching, as if trying to decide whether to trust her. And then, for the first time since they had met, he let his guard down—truly down. His shoulders relaxed, his eyes softened, and he let out a breath he had been holding for what felt like years.

"I want to try," he said, his voice low but steady. "I don't know how to love, Sophia. But I want to try."

The relief that washed over her was overwhelming. It wasn't everything—there was still so much they needed to work through—but it was a start. A real start.

"Thank you," she whispered, her eyes filling with unshed tears. "That's all I've ever wanted."

They sat in silence for a while, holding hands across the table as the sun dipped below the horizon, casting the world in a deep, comforting twilight. The walls between them, once so impenetrable, were slowly falling away, brick by brick.

That night, for the first time, Aris didn't retreat to his separate room. He stayed with her, not out of obligation, but out of choice. They lay in bed together, not touching, but close enough that Sophia could feel the warmth of his presence. It was a small step, but it meant everything.

As she drifted off to sleep, Sophia realized that, for the first time since their marriage, she felt a glimmer of hope. They still had a long way to go, but for the first time, she believed they could make it. Together.

9

A NEW BEGINNING

The soft morning light filtered through the windows of the villa, casting a warm glow over the room. For the first time in what felt like forever, Sophia awoke with a sense of calm. She stretched in bed, feeling the cool sheets beneath her fingertips, but more importantly, feeling the presence of Aris beside her. Though they hadn't touched during the night, the simple fact that he had stayed meant more to her than words could express.

She turned her head slightly, watching him sleep. His face was relaxed, the usual tension gone, and for a moment, he didn't look like the guarded man she had married. He looked human, vulnerable, and at peace. A part of her wanted to reach out and brush the hair from his forehead, to touch him and confirm that this change was real, but she held back, not wanting to break the quiet moment.

The weight of their conversation the night before lingered in the air, but it no longer felt heavy. Instead, there was a lightness, a sense that maybe—just maybe—they were finally on the same path. Aris had opened up to her in a way she hadn't thought possible, admitting his fears, his struggles.

And for the first time, she felt that he truly saw her, not just as a convenient wife but as a partner, someone he was beginning to trust.

As she slipped out of bed to make coffee, she marveled at how quickly things had shifted between them. There was still so much left unsaid, so much they needed to work through, but the fact that they had taken this first step gave her hope.

Aris stirred as she moved about the kitchen, blinking against the sunlight as he sat up. His eyes found her across the room, and for a moment, neither of them spoke. Then, as if something unspoken passed between them, he gave her a small, hesitant smile.

"Morning," he said, his voice a little rough from sleep.

"Good morning," she replied, her own smile matching his as she poured two cups of coffee.

He got out of bed, pulling on a light robe before crossing the room to join her. The ease of the morning was unfamiliar but welcome. There was no awkwardness, no tension hanging between them like before. Aris accepted the cup she handed him, his fingers brushing hers, and though it was a simple touch, it sent warmth spiraling through her.

"About last night…" Aris began, his voice hesitant, as if he wasn't sure how to continue.

Sophia met his gaze, sensing the importance of what he was about to say. She took a breath, preparing herself. "You don't have to explain. I understand."

But Aris shook his head. "No, I do need to explain." He set his coffee down, running a hand through his tousled hair. "What I said, about not knowing how to love… it's true. I've spent my whole life building this wall around myself because I didn't think I needed anyone. But now, I realize how much I've hurt you by keeping you out. And I don't want to do that anymore."

Sophia's heart swelled at his words. She could hear the sincerity in his voice, and it meant everything. She stepped closer, her voice soft. "It's not too late, Aris. We can still figure this out. Together."

He looked down at her, his dark eyes filled with something she hadn't seen before—hope. "I want that, Sophia. I want to try, not just for you, but for us. I can't promise I'll be perfect, but I'll do my best."

She reached for his hand, threading her fingers through his. "That's all I need."

The vulnerability in that moment was new for both of them, but it felt like the start of something real. For the first time, they weren't just two people bound by circumstance— they were partners, standing on the same ground, willing to face the unknown together.

The rest of the day passed in a blur of exploration. They wandered through the winding streets of Santorini, visiting small artisan shops, enjoying the local food, and soaking in the beauty of the island. It wasn't a grand, romantic gesture, but the simplicity of it made it even more meaningful. Every time Aris reached for her hand, every glance they exchanged, felt like a step toward something deeper.

In the late afternoon, they found themselves sitting on a secluded beach, the waves lapping at their feet as they watched the sun begin its slow descent toward the horizon. The world around them was quiet, the chaos of their past few days seeming far away.

"I don't know why it took me so long to realize this," Aris said, his voice quiet but clear, "but being with you... it's not something I want to lose. I know I said I could never love you, but now... I'm not sure if that's true anymore."

Sophia's breath caught in her throat. His words hung in

the air, filling the space between them with a possibility she hadn't dared to hope for.

"Aris…" she whispered, her heart pounding.

He turned to her, his expression serious, but there was something softer in his eyes now. "I don't know if I'm ready to say I love you, but I know I feel something. And I want to figure out what that is."

Tears pricked at the corners of her eyes, but she blinked them away, not wanting to ruin the moment. "That's all I ever wanted. Just for you to be open to the possibility."

He reached out, cupping her cheek with a tenderness she hadn't expected, his thumb brushing away a tear she hadn't realized had fallen. "I don't deserve you, Sophia," he murmured. "But I'm going to spend every day trying to."

She leaned into his touch, her heart swelling with emotions she couldn't put into words. "We'll figure it out," she whispered, her voice filled with the quiet confidence of someone who finally believed things could change.

As the sun set over the Aegean, casting a brilliant array of colors across the sky, Aris leaned in and kissed her. It wasn't the kiss of a man bound by duty—it was the kiss of a man who was beginning to see the woman in front of him for who she truly was, and for the first time, letting her see him, too.

This wasn't the end of their story. It was only the beginning of something new—a partnership built on honesty, vulnerability, and the hope that love, once thought impossible, might just be within reach.

THE FAMILY STRUGGLE

Returning to Athens after the honeymoon was a stark reminder of the world they had left behind. The quiet intimacy they had begun to build in Santorini seemed to fade the moment they stepped foot in the Kostas family estate. The sprawling mansion, with its towering columns and ornate décor, was a symbol of everything that had kept them apart for so long—expectations, duty, and appearances.

Sophia felt a tightening in her chest as they were greeted by the Kostas family's ever-watchful staff. The house hummed with the same controlled order that had always made her feel like an outsider. And then there was Eleni Kostas, Aris' mother, waiting for them at the top of the grand staircase, her sharp eyes taking in every detail as they approached.

"Sophia, Aris," Eleni said, her voice cool but polite. "Welcome back. I trust your honeymoon was… satisfactory?"

Sophia managed a smile, though she felt Eleni's gaze piercing through her, as if searching for any cracks in the marriage. "It was beautiful," she replied, keeping her tone steady. "Santorini was perfect."

Eleni's expression didn't change, but her eyes flicked toward Aris. "Good. Now that you're back, there are matters that need your attention, Aris. The business requires your focus. I've been managing things in your absence, but some issues can only be handled by you."

Sophia sensed the shift in Aris the moment his mother mentioned the business. His posture straightened, and the warmth she had felt from him during their honeymoon seemed to drain away, replaced by the familiar coldness of the billionaire heir. "I'll attend to them first thing tomorrow," he said, his voice all business.

Eleni nodded, satisfied, before turning her gaze to Sophia once more. "And you, Sophia, I trust you'll adjust back to life here without any issues. The Kostas family has certain expectations for its members, and I'm sure you'll continue to uphold them."

The unspoken words hung in the air—don't forget your place. Sophia forced another smile, nodding as if she understood exactly what was expected of her. "Of course."

With that, Eleni dismissed herself, leaving Sophia and Aris standing alone in the grand entryway. The silence between them felt heavier than it had in days.

"She still sees me as an outsider," Sophia said quietly, her voice barely audible as they began walking toward their wing of the house.

Aris sighed, running a hand through his hair. "She's always been like that—rigid, focused on the family's legacy above all else. It's not about you, Sophia. It's about control. She's used to running everything, and now that I'm taking over more of the business, she's clinging to whatever power she can."

Sophia appreciated Aris' attempt to explain, but it didn't make Eleni's scrutiny any easier to bear. She had always known marrying into the Kostas family would come with challenges, but she hadn't realized just how much Eleni would loom over their lives, constantly watching, constantly judging.

"She'll never accept me, will she?" Sophia asked, her voice tinged with frustration.

Aris stopped walking and turned to face her, his expression softening as he placed a hand on her arm. "She'll come around. She'll have to. You're my wife now, and I won't let her interfere with our lives."

Sophia searched his eyes, wanting to believe him, but the weight of Eleni's presence was impossible to ignore. Still, there was a quiet strength in Aris' words that gave her a small measure of comfort.

But as the days passed, the pressures of the business quickly consumed Aris. Meetings, phone calls, and endless paperwork pulled him deeper into the world he had been raised to dominate. Sophia could feel him slipping away, retreating behind the walls of responsibility that had kept him distant for so long.

One evening, after a particularly long day of meetings, Aris returned to their private suite, his face drawn with exhaustion. He collapsed into the chair by the fireplace, rubbing his temples as if trying to stave off a headache.

Sophia watched him from across the room, her heart aching at the sight of him so worn down. She crossed the space between them and knelt by his side, placing a hand on his knee.

"Aris," she said softly, "you're working yourself too hard."

He sighed, looking down at her with tired eyes. "There's too much to do. The business... there are problems that need fixing. I don't have a choice."

Sophia shook her head. "There's always a choice. You don't have to do this alone. I'm here, Aris. Let me help."

He looked at her, his expression softening at her words, but there was a flicker of doubt in his eyes. "I don't want you to get caught up in all of this. The business, the pressure—it's not what you signed up for."

"I signed up for you," Sophia said firmly. "I knew what this life would be like, and I'm not afraid of it. But I can't stand by and watch you burn yourself out. Let me in, Aris. Let me be your partner, not just in name, but in everything."

Aris exhaled, his hand coming up to rest over hers. For a long moment, he said nothing, the silence between them filled with the weight of his unspoken fears. But then, finally, he nodded. "I don't know how to let go of control," he admitted quietly. "It's all I've ever known."

Sophia smiled gently, her heart swelling with love for this man who was trying so hard to break free from the expectations that had been placed on him for so long. "You don't have to let go completely," she said. "Just let me share the burden with you. We're in this together."

Aris leaned forward, resting his forehead against hers, his breath warm against her skin. "Thank you," he whispered, his voice filled with gratitude and vulnerability. "I don't know what I'd do without you."

Sophia closed her eyes, savoring the moment, the closeness between them that had taken so long to build. "You'll never have to find out."

As the days turned into weeks, Aris began to open up more, allowing Sophia to be a part of the business decisions and the pressures he had once shouldered alone. It wasn't easy—there were moments when he struggled to let go of control, moments when he slipped back into old habits—but slowly, they found a rhythm. Together, they began to navigate the complexities of their world, not as two individuals bound by duty, but as partners, united in their struggles and their hopes for the future.

Eleni's disapproval still lingered, but Sophia no longer let it define her. She had Aris now, and they were building something real—something that went beyond the expectations of their families or the demands of their legacy. For the first time, Sophia felt that she was truly part of this life, not just a bystander.

And as for Aris, he began to realize that love wasn't a weakness, but a strength. He hadn't known how to love before, but now, with Sophia by his side, he was learning. And in that learning, he was finding a new kind of freedom— a freedom that came from letting someone in, from sharing the weight of his world with the one person who understood him better than anyone else.

Their life together wasn't perfect, and it never would be. But it was theirs, and that was enough.

11

A TEST OF LOVE

Weeks passed, and the partnership Sophia and Aris were building continued to grow stronger, but life within the Kostas empire was never without its complications. The Kostas business, sprawling and powerful, had weathered many storms, but now, a new one loomed on the horizon. A scandal was brewing—one that could threaten everything Aris had worked so hard to protect.

The first signs came quietly, whispers in the media about mismanagement in one of the family's shipping ventures. At first, Aris brushed them off as rumors, but it didn't take long for the situation to escalate. Soon, accusations of corruption began circulating, and an investigation was launched, placing the entire Kostas fortune under scrutiny.

Sophia watched Aris as the weight of the scandal began to take its toll on him. His late nights in the office grew even later, and his shoulders carried a tension that seemed impossible to release. He was trying to keep her out of it, trying to protect her from the ugliness of the business world, but Sophia wasn't willing to be kept in the dark.

One evening, after Aris had spent hours locked away in

his study, Sophia decided it was time to confront him. She knocked gently on the door before pushing it open, finding him seated at his desk, his head in his hands. Papers and files were strewn across the desk, evidence of the chaos that had taken over their lives.

"Aris," she said softly, stepping into the room. "You can't keep doing this. You can't keep shutting me out."

He looked up at her, his face drawn with exhaustion. "Sophia, I'm trying to keep you away from this mess. It's not your fight."

"It is my fight," she insisted, walking over to him. "I'm your wife. We're in this together. You promised we'd be partners, remember? Let me help."

Aris leaned back in his chair, rubbing his eyes. "I don't want you to get dragged into this. It's ugly, Sophia. The press, the investigators, the board—they're all circling like vultures. And if things go wrong, the whole company could be in jeopardy."

Sophia knelt in front of him, her eyes locking onto his. "I don't care about the company. I care about you. You can't carry all of this alone. Let me stand with you."

Aris exhaled sharply, the tension in his body palpable. For a long moment, he said nothing, his mind clearly wrestling with the decision. Then, slowly, he nodded. "Alright," he said quietly. "You're right. I can't do this alone."

Sophia reached for his hand, giving it a reassuring squeeze. "We'll get through this, Aris. Together."

The next few days were a whirlwind. Meetings with lawyers, crisis management teams, and the company's board of directors consumed their time. Sophia was by Aris' side every step of the way, offering her support, her insight, and her strength. Together, they faced the mounting pressure, the media scrutiny, and the uncertainty that hung over their future.

But the stress took its toll, and there were moments when the cracks in their relationship threatened to resurface. Aris, despite his best efforts, struggled to relinquish control. He had spent his entire life being the one in charge, the one who fixed problems, and letting Sophia in—truly letting her in—was harder than he had imagined.

One night, after an especially grueling meeting with the company's legal team, Aris lashed out in frustration.

"I can't believe this is happening," he said, pacing the length of their living room. "One mistake, one misstep, and everything I've worked for could be gone. How did it get this bad?"

Sophia watched him from the sofa, her heart aching at the sight of him so consumed by anger and fear. "Aris," she said softly, "we'll find a way through this. You've built this company with integrity. The truth will come out."

He stopped pacing, turning to face her with a look of helplessness she hadn't seen before. "What if the truth isn't enough?" he asked, his voice tight. "What if I can't fix this?"

Sophia stood and crossed the room to him, placing her hands on his arms. "Then we face it together. But you have to trust me, Aris. You have to let me help, not just with the business, but with you. You can't keep pushing me away when things get hard."

Aris looked down at her, his expression conflicted. "I'm not used to this, Sophia. I'm not used to needing anyone."

"I know," she said gently. "But you don't have to do this alone anymore. You have me. You always will."

For a moment, Aris was silent, his eyes searching hers as if looking for reassurance. And then, slowly, he nodded. "I'm trying," he whispered, his voice filled with a vulnerability that made her heart ache. "I'm trying so hard, but I don't know if it's enough."

Sophia reached up, cupping his face in her hands. "It's enough, Aris. You're enough."

In that moment, something shifted between them. The walls that had once stood so tall between them were crumbling, and Aris, for the first time, was letting her in completely. He wrapped his arms around her, pulling her close, and Sophia could feel the weight of his fears, his burdens, in the way he held her.

"I'm scared," he admitted, his voice barely above a whisper. "I'm scared of losing everything."

Sophia rested her head against his chest, her heart aching for him. "You won't lose everything," she said softly. "No matter what happens, you have me. We'll figure this out."

They stood like that for a long time, wrapped in each other's arms, the silence between them filled with unspoken promises. Aris had spent his whole life believing that love was a weakness, that needing someone meant losing control. But now, as he held Sophia, he realized that letting her in, allowing himself to need her, wasn't weakness at all.

It was strength.

The next morning, they faced the board together. The accusations were daunting, the scandal threatening to destroy the company's reputation, but Sophia stood by Aris' side, her presence a steadying force. With her support, Aris confronted the challenges head-on, refusing to let fear or doubt cloud his judgment.

And when the truth finally came out—that the scandal had been the result of a rogue employee's actions, not Aris' mismanagement—the relief was palpable. The company was safe, the storm had passed, and the Kostas legacy remained intact.

As they left the boardroom, Aris turned to Sophia, his hand squeezing hers tightly. "Thank you," he said quietly, his eyes filled with gratitude. "I couldn't have done this without you."

Sophia smiled up at him, her heart full. "You never have to do it alone again, Aris."

And in that moment, as they walked out of the building, hand in hand, Aris knew that he had finally found something far more valuable than power or control.

He had found love.

12

THE RECKONING

The relief that swept over the Kostas family after the scandal was immense, but it left both Aris and Sophia changed. For Aris, it had been a stark reminder that control could slip through his fingers no matter how tightly he held on. For Sophia, it solidified her belief that they were stronger together. The tension that had once defined their marriage was now replaced by a sense of unity, but the challenges weren't entirely over.

After the board cleared Aris of any wrongdoing, the media shifted their focus to another story: his marriage to Sophia. Questions about their relationship began to surface, with the tabloids suggesting that their union had been nothing more than a business arrangement. The scrutiny put even more pressure on their newly mended relationship, and once again, the Kostas family was thrust into the public eye.

Aris, determined to protect Sophia from the invasive speculation, decided to take matters into his own hands. "We need to end this," he said one evening, pacing the length of their living room as Sophia watched from the sofa. His frustration was palpable, his jaw clenched as he scanned the latest headlines. "The media is relentless. They're picking apart every aspect of our marriage."

Sophia set down the magazine she'd been pretending to read and sighed. "I know. But we can't control what they say, Aris. All we can do is show them that we're not what they think."

Aris stopped pacing and looked at her, his eyes softening. "And how do we do that? They won't leave us alone until they find something to destroy."

She stood and crossed the room to him, reaching for his hands. "We show them the truth. Not with grand gestures, not with staged interviews, but by being ourselves. By showing them we're not just a business deal, but two people who care about each other. We've come too far to let them tear us apart now."

Aris squeezed her hands, his expression conflicted. "I don't want you to have to face this."

"I'm not afraid of them," Sophia said, her voice steady. "I'm only afraid of losing what we've built."

His eyes softened, and he pulled her into his arms, holding her close. "You won't lose me. I promise."

The next day, Aris called a press conference—something he had avoided for as long as possible. It was a risky move, but it was time to face the rumors head-on. The media had painted him as the cold, detached billionaire who had married out of convenience, and they had cast Sophia as a woman trapped in a loveless marriage. It was a narrative neither of them could accept anymore.

The press conference was held in the courtyard of the Kostas estate, with reporters gathered, their cameras and microphones ready. Aris and Sophia stood side by side, their hands intertwined, a united front against the onslaught of questions.

One reporter, bold and blunt, asked the question everyone had been whispering. "Mr. Kostas, your marriage has been called a business transaction. Can you explain why you chose to marry Sophia?"

Aris glanced at Sophia, his grip on her hand tightening ever so slightly. For a moment, he hesitated, the familiar instinct to maintain his guarded exterior creeping in. But then he looked back at the crowd, his voice steady and clear.

"I married Sophia because I need her," he said, the weight of his words hanging in the air. "Not because of business or duty, but because she makes me better. I've spent most of my life believing I didn't need anyone, that love was a distraction. But I was wrong."

The reporters exchanged surprised glances, their pens scribbling furiously as Aris continued.

"Sophia taught me that love isn't a weakness—it's a strength. She stood by me when I was too proud to ask for help, and she's shown me what it means to truly let someone in. This marriage is real, and it's the best decision I've ever made."

Sophia's heart swelled at his words. She had never heard him speak so openly, especially in front of so many people. For so long, Aris had kept his emotions buried deep, but now, he was baring his soul for the world to see.

The reporters weren't done yet, though. One of them turned to Sophia. "And you, Mrs. Kostas? There have been rumors that you were pressured into this marriage. Can you confirm or deny that?"

Sophia smiled, calm and composed. "I wasn't pressured into anything," she said firmly. "This marriage started as a way to help both our families, yes. But what we've built goes far beyond that. Aris and I have been through more than most people could imagine, and we've come out stronger. I love him, and that's not something that can be bought or arranged."

The press conference continued for another few minutes, but the questions became softer, less accusatory. By the end, Sophia and Aris had walked away from the scrutiny with their heads held high, their relationship finally on their terms —not defined by the media, the Kostas family, or anyone else.

Later that evening, as they sat together on the balcony overlooking the city, the weight of the day began to lift. The night was warm, the air thick with the scent of jasmine, and the twinkling lights of Athens stretched out before them like a sea of stars.

"I didn't expect you to say all that," Sophia said softly, leaning her head on Aris' shoulder. "You were amazing."

Aris wrapped an arm around her, pulling her close. "I meant every word. I'm done hiding how I feel. From now on, we face everything together. No more walls between us."

Sophia smiled, feeling a sense of peace she hadn't felt in months. "I can't believe how far we've come."

Aris kissed the top of her head, his voice tender. "And we've still got a long way to go. But as long as we're together, I know we can handle anything."

They sat in comfortable silence for a while, the soft hum of the city below creating a peaceful backdrop. For the first time in a long time, the future felt bright—uncertain, yes, but full of possibility.

As the night deepened, Aris turned to her, a serious look in his eyes. "Sophia, I have something I need to tell you."

Her heart skipped a beat. "What is it?"

He took her hands in his, his expression filled with a mixture of nerves and affection. "I told you I didn't know if I could ever love you, and I'm sorry I ever said that. Because the truth is, I do love you. I think I've loved you for longer than I realized. I was just too afraid to admit it."

Sophia's breath caught in her throat, her eyes welling up with tears. "Aris…"

He smiled, a rare softness in his gaze. "I love you, Sophia. And I'm not afraid to say it anymore."

Tears spilled down her cheeks as she threw her arms around him, holding him tightly. "I love you too," she whispered, her voice thick with emotion. "So much."

They held each other under the stars, the weight of everything they had been through falling away. Their journey had been long and difficult, but they had found their way to each other. And in that moment, they knew that whatever the future held, they would face it together.

Their love was real, and it was enough.

13

HAPPILY EVER AFTER?

Months passed, and life settled into a rhythm for Aris and Sophia. The scandal that had once threatened to destroy the Kostas empire was now a distant memory, and their relationship had evolved into something deeper and more meaningful than either of them had expected. They weren't just husband and wife—they were partners in every sense of the word. The walls Aris had once built so high were gone, replaced by trust and love that had been hard-earned.

The media, having finally accepted that their marriage was real, had moved on to other stories. The Kostas name was no longer in the tabloids, and the constant scrutiny had faded. Sophia felt a sense of peace that she hadn't experienced since marrying into the powerful family. Life wasn't perfect—there were still challenges with the business, and Eleni Kostas still kept a watchful eye on them—but those challenges now felt manageable.

Sophia had also found her place in the business, working alongside Aris to ensure that the company continued to thrive. It wasn't something she had planned for herself, but she discovered she had a knack for navigating the complexities of the corporate world. Aris had been impressed with her insights, and slowly, she had earned the respect of the board and the employees, not just as the wife of the CEO, but as a force of her own.

One evening, as they prepared to host a grand gala at their estate—an event to celebrate a new partnership that would expand the Kostas empire into new markets—Sophia stood in front of the mirror, adjusting the elegant gown she wore. The soft, flowing fabric shimmered under the lights, and she felt more confident than ever.

Aris entered the room, already dressed in his tuxedo. He paused when he saw her, his eyes lingering on her reflection in the mirror. A smile spread across his face, the same one that still made her heart skip a beat. "You look beautiful," he said softly, stepping toward her.

Sophia smiled back, turning to face him. "Thank you. You don't look too bad yourself."

He chuckled, placing his hands on her waist. "Are you ready for tonight?"

She took a deep breath, nodding. "I think so. It's a big night, but we've handled worse."

Aris kissed her gently, his lips brushing hers. "I'm proud of you, you know. For everything. You've become more than I ever could have imagined. I couldn't have gotten through any of this without you."

Sophia's heart swelled at his words. She had never imagined she would hear something like that from Aris, the man who had once been so closed off, so focused on his duty that he couldn't see anything beyond it. Now, here he was, standing before her, telling her that she had changed his life.

"I'm proud of you too," she said, resting her forehead

against his. "Look how far we've come. From where we started... it's hard to believe."

Aris's eyes softened, and he pulled her closer. "It's been a journey, hasn't it?"

"A long one," she replied, laughing softly. "But worth every step."

The night unfolded in a whirlwind of laughter, music, and celebration. The Kostas estate was filled with guests, from business partners to close friends, and the atmosphere was one of joy and success. Sophia moved through the crowd with ease, greeting guests and making sure everything ran smoothly. It was a world she had once felt alien in, but now, she belonged.

As the evening wore on, Sophia found herself standing on the terrace, looking out over the estate's sprawling gardens, which were lit with twinkling lights. The soft hum of the party drifted in the background, but out here, it was peaceful. Aris joined her, slipping his arm around her waist as they gazed out at the scene.

"It's beautiful," Sophia said, her voice full of contentment.

Aris nodded. "It is. But not as beautiful as you."

She turned to him, smiling. "Always the charmer."

He grinned, leaning in to kiss her. When he pulled back, there was a serious look in his eyes. "There's something I've been meaning to ask you."

Sophia raised an eyebrow, curious. "What is it?"

He hesitated for a moment, then took both of her hands in his, his gaze never leaving hers. "We've built something amazing together, Sophia. More than I ever thought possible. But there's one thing missing."

Her heart began to race, wondering what he could be talking about. "What do you mean?"

Aris's smile softened, and he took a deep breath. "I want to start a family with you."

The words hit her like a wave, filling her with warmth and excitement. She had thought about it before, but with everything they had been through, it had always seemed like something for the distant future. Now, standing here with Aris, hearing him say it out loud, made it feel real.

"You do?" she asked, her voice soft.

He nodded, his eyes full of love. "I want it more than anything. I want to build a future with you—not just for the business or the family name, but for us. For the life we've created together."

Sophia felt tears welling up in her eyes, but they were tears of joy. She smiled through them, squeezing his hands tightly. "I want that too, Aris. I want everything with you."

He pulled her into his arms, holding her close, and in that moment, Sophia knew that this was her happily ever after. It wasn't the fairy tale she had once imagined—there had been hardships, heartbreaks, and challenges along the way—but it was real, and it was hers. She had found love with a man who had once believed he could never love, and together, they had built something strong and lasting.

As the music from the party played softly in the background, Aris kissed her again, sealing their promise of a future together. They stood on the terrace, wrapped in each other's arms, ready to face whatever came next—knowing that, no matter what, they would face it together.

And that was more than enough.

EPILOGUE: A LEGACY OF LOVE

Several years later, Aris and Sophia stood in the same garden where they had once promised each other a future. Their daughter, a bright-eyed little girl with her father's dark hair and her mother's smile, ran through the flowers, laughing as she chased the butterflies that danced around her.

Aris watched her with a soft smile, then turned to Sophia, slipping his arm around her waist. "She's perfect, isn't she?"

Sophia leaned into him, her heart full. "She is. Just like her father."

He chuckled, kissing the top of her head. "And just like her mother."

As they stood together, watching their daughter play, Sophia felt a deep sense of peace. Their journey hadn't been easy, but it had led them here—to a life filled with love, family, and the promise of a future they had built together.

They had found their happily ever after, not in the way the world had expected, but in a way that was entirely their own.

And it was perfect.

*** THE END ***

AUTHOR'S NOTE

Dear Reader,

Thank you for picking up *Love in Greece*. This story is a labor of love—a tale of second chances, breaking down walls, and discovering that love, even in the unlikeliest of places, can bloom in the most beautiful ways.

Aris and Sophia's journey is one of growth, vulnerability, and trust. I wanted to explore what happens when two people who seem worlds apart are brought together by circumstance and forced to confront not only each other but the parts of themselves they've kept hidden for far too long.

The breathtaking backdrop of Greece felt like the perfect setting for a story about passion and possibility. Its timeless beauty and rich history mirror the timeless struggles of love, duty, and the human heart.

As you read, I hope you felt l swept away by the romance, the drama, and the triumph of love over fear. I hope Aris and Sophia's story will remind you that even when life feels uncertain, love can be the anchor that holds us steady and the light that guides us forward.

Thank you for taking this journey with me. Your support

means the world, and I'm so grateful to share this story with you.

With all my love,
Mollie

P.S. If you enjoy Love in Greece, please consider leaving a review—it helps other readers discover this story and brings so much joy to authors like me! 🖤

Read on, for an excerpt from *Love in Venice*, my award-winning romance from the *True Love* series. Each story can be read as a stand alone novel

If you'd like to learn more about these characters, gain inside tips into the writing process, or be the first to know when a new book is released, subscribe to my newsletter here: http://eepurl.com/ghM501

Please email me and I'll be in touch personally—I promise...mollie@molliemathews.com.

EXCERPT LOVE IN VENICE

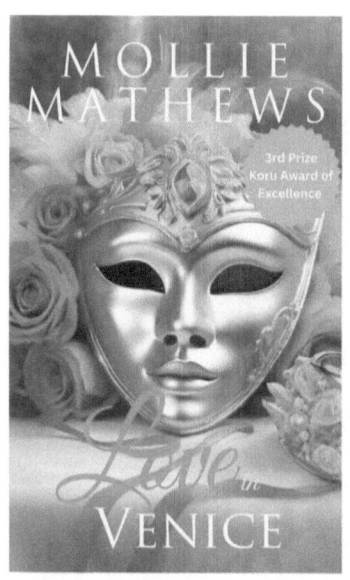

Third-place Award-winner in the Romance Writers of New Zealand Koru awards, recognising excellence in romance writing! Readers around the world judge this award. Thank you!

CHAPTER ONE

"**D**o I have to order you to take time off, Margaret?" Dr Elizabeth Buckley carefully folded her stethoscope and gestured for Maggie to get dressed before returning grimly to her desk. "Make no mistake, it's not a case of if you will suffer a heart attack. It's when you will suffer one."

She briefly thumbed through her medical file while waiting for Maggie to return to her chair. As she sat down before her, she looked up from reading through her medical history and leant toward her. Her green eyes flashed accusingly at her, and her delicate blonde eyebrows burrowed deeply.

"I know you mean well, Liz, but I can't take time off now. All I need is one more month to pull this deal together. So much is at stake. The reality is that if I quit now, I may as well call it a day."

"I wish I could help, Maggie. But, I'm urging you not just as a friend but as your Doctor – your blood pressure is through the roof, your heartbeat is erratic, and you're adrenalised to the max. It's a miracle you haven't collapsed."

"it's true. I've been working hard. But it will return to normal in one month, and I can relax. "

"I don't think you realise how serious this is, Maggie. You seem to be under the illusion that your heart is something you can control. You can think you buy yourself an extra month. Well, Maggie Green, I've got news for you. You can endure more stress than the average person, but even you have limitations."

"What do you suggest I do? Chuck everything I've worked for in and sit under a tree somewhere meditating?" she said crossly.

"Don't be so dramatic. You've been telling yourself that workaholic story all your life. It's time to tell yourself a new story—one with plenty of chapters about rest. Take a break, put your feet up, and go somewhere nice, somewhere you've always wanted to go but could never find the time. You've changed recently. I've noticed it. We all have. Quite frankly, I'm worried about you, Maggie. You've lost your sparkle, your humour. You've lost you. You've become so brittle and short-tempered. I don't mean to be unkind; I'm saying this as your friend."

The words stung, biting into the fragile core of her self-esteem. She hated criticism, but this time the words especially hurt. It was true. Dr Buckley was summing up what she had always feared. She was brittle, hardhearted, uncaring, and unlovable. She fought back tears and slumped back in her chair.

"Do yourself a favour, take time off, recharge, rediscover the Maggie I used to know. The Maggie we all love."

"All right."

"Promise me?"

"Yes, I promise." Maggie got up dejectedly and made her way to the door. She walked out of her office into the cool

Manhattan air. As she merged with the busy pedestrian high-way, swimming with New York's most successful elite, the reality of her situation hit with a thud.

She, Maggie Green, Ms Invincible, was burnt out.

Her health was at risk, and other than Dr Elizabeth Buck-ley, nobody cared. Everything she had worked so hard for suddenly seemed insignificant. The reality was that other than her work, she had nothing.

Nothing and nobody.

It would be alone if she were to go away, as incredible as the notion was.

CHAPTER TWO

M aggie had heard Venice was beautiful, but nothing prepared her for the flood of emotions that overwhelmed her as she stepped from the train station and saw the Grand Canal for the first time three days after leaving New York.

It was such a relief to arrive safely, and as she took in the magical, heart-wrenching view, a lifetime of stress melted away. The beauty of Venice struck her as soon as she arrived, and the symphony of sounds that permeated the air instantly transported her to a past where life was simple, and beauty was revered. It was so unlike New York, where she felt that the modern, not the antique, was glorified. Where she felt only as good as her last deal.

She heaved a great sigh of relief, grateful to have left her life momentarily behind. One month would go quickly enough in most places, but it would seem like a lifetime here.

"We should be able to see this place in a few hours," she overheard a man say to his wife. "There's nothing but a few churches and a lot of water."

She looked at the couple with pity. She felt sorry for their ignorance about all the sights to be seen, the exotic places to go, and the inspirational art to experience first-hand. Maggie, as always, had been thorough in her research—and with good reason. It had been years since she had pursued her life-long interest in art history. Not since—

She quickly changed her thoughts. She didn't want to think about him. She didn't want to revisit memories that only triggered trauma. All she knew was that her dreams had become whims, fantasies only the idle or extraordinarily wealthy could indulge.

Hard work was the road to salvation, she silently affirmed. Her mother had drummed that into her. Maggie Green knew what it was to work hard and sacrifice her needs. For years she had faithfully played the dutiful daughter, boss, sister, and doormat to the masses.

But not now. Not now that she was on a forced sabbatical. Not now, in this beautiful place, where passions which had long lain dormant were spontaneously set free. Not now that her deepest longings soared high above worldly concerns like doves set free against a peaceful blue sky.

Maggie felt invigorated and ready for new adventures. But she would keep her feet firmly on the ground, she reminded herself, averting her gaze to avoid the amorous glances of a far-too-cliched, far-too-handsome Italian man.

Maggie had been warned to be wary of Italian stallions who looked like modern-day cupids, with masses of shiny black curls and boyish faces.

"Watch out for the ones who ask you if you're an artist," her long-time friend and motivational life coach, Chanel, had warned her. "Like a love-starved fool, I fell for their charms, hook, line and lead pencil. Before I knew it, I was being led through twisting narrow streets to what they promised was their own artist's gallery, only to be pinned to the wall in a passionate declaration of love."

Maggie had at first been horrified and then confused.

Chanel had giggled and added, "Actually, it was all rather exciting! I just adored him. He was like my very own Michelangelo, and let's be honest—New Yorkers aren't the most passionate men. A woman needs what a woman needs—and what you need, Maggie is a really good bonk. It would do you a world of good. Let your hair down, lighten up a little, and make wild passionate love a lot!"

"Thanks for the tip, Chanel. I'll try and remember that," Maggie had said politely, her jaw clenching and chills running down her spine. The idea of a romantic liaison, especially with a foreign man, left her cold. She had her reasons, good reasons, and ones she didn't intend to share.

Not with anyone. Thank God she had got rid of the evidence.

CHAPTER THREE

A violent tug on the sleeve of Maggie's dress startled her. She turned around angrily, cross at the intrusion and furious that someone should roughly finger the new black velvet Dolce and Gabbana dress she had purchased for her first trip to Venice.

She flicked back her hair, allowing the heavy curtain of blonde locks to cascade down her back until they settled upon her shoulder blades. Her green eyes narrowed wildly, and her lips pursed crossly. Maggie Green was a formidable opponent and someone not to be messed with.

Her face softened as she looked down at the young girl standing before her.

"*Scusi, Senora*, please help me," the girl pleaded, forcing a bunch of perfectly shaped red roses toward Maggie.

Maggie stepped back suddenly to avoid being scratched by the stiff, long-stemmed blooms and turned to walk away.

The girl with roses followed. She overtook Maggie and looked up at her with pleading eyes, the colour and sheen of melting chocolate. "Only three euros."

Her dull, dark hair sprung around her pale, gaunt face in

mottled curls. Huge, round eyes with the longest lashes Maggie had ever seen peered past her carefully fortified barrier and burrowed into Maggie's soul.

She could have been just another girl begging for money if not for her bulging stomach and the small bundle she carried in her arms. Maggie felt unusually sympathetic toward her.

She wondered how old this girl was and roughly guessed her age to be 14. Too young, Maggie thought sadly, to be raising a child.

She knew her situation intimately. She was not much older when her father had walked out on her mother, leaving behind her and her five younger siblings.

Maggie's childhood ended abruptly as her mother sunk into depression and sought comfort from the icy cold waters of Gordon's gin and the warm bloody lakes of cardboard merlot.

It seemed a matter of course that Maggie, as the oldest, should take over raising her younger brothers and sisters. Only Maggie's fiery nature and dogged determination helped her endure the long hours that working by day and studying by night involved.

A lot of water had passed over the road, and now 25 years later, Maggie was a qualified corporate lawyer and managing director of a large international consultancy firm. Looking down at the scruffy girl beside her, she doubted that life would work out so well for her.

The young woman persevered, pushing the bunch of red roses toward Maggie again. "For my family," she said, gesturing to the bundle in her arms and rubbing a hand on her stomach.

Maggie admired the girl's persistence and wish to provide for her family. Perhaps she wouldn't have believed the girl if she had been in New York. But in Venice, everything took on a rosy glow, and even she, renowned by others as hard-hearted and guarded, felt unusually trusting. Venice was too powerful a seductress, its beauty and mystique too evocative.

Intoxicated by the gilded gondola traversing the Grand Canal, the beauty of the palazzos and churches hugging its shores, and the dancing light that illuminated all the surfaces it touched, Maggie opened her heart.

As she placed her suitcases on the cobbled street, she wondered what difference giving twenty Euros to the young pregnant girl would make. She knew it was far more than the roses were worth. Instead, she decided it would be good to be extra generous and settled on 50 Euros, the equivalent of 100 USD.

As she unclasped her Chanel handbag, the young girl threw the bundle she had held at Maggie. Maggie reached out instinctively to catch it. As the bundle, which Maggie thought was the girl's baby, flew through the air, she snatched Maggie's purse from her hands.

Three roughly dressed men with oily black hair suddenly appeared from the depths of the crowd.

One of them pushed Maggie forcibly to one side. Another roughly swept her suitcases from the pavement and ran at high speed away from her, snaking their way through the bulging crowd.

It happened so quickly that she didn't have time to react. She struggled to regain her balance, powerless to do anything. She wanted to run after them. A man's hand, firmly placed on her shoulder, stopped her in her tracks. A shiver went down her spine.

"Do not move!" A well-educated, Italian voice said in perfect English. "Wait. It is too dangerous."

Maggie momentarily glimpsed a tall, muscular, well-dressed man running toward the thieves.

"*Arrestili! Arrestili!* Stop them!" He called urgently in English and Italian as he pushed through the crowd.

A wave of pain surged through Maggie. She clutched her chest. "I can't...can't...can't breathe," she gasped, her face contorting as her lungs constricted.

She was barely aware of the crowd of concerned people drawing closer as her eyes flickered and she drifted in and out of consciousness. Her head felt dizzy. Her legs felt numb. Her heart felt dead. She struggled to maintain her balance. Unable to fight losing consciousness, she surrendered to the darkness that descended like a heavy velvet curtain.

A splash of water suddenly brought her back to life. She awoke to find the tall, dark, arrestingly handsome stranger's concerned face staring down at her. She temporarily lost herself in the depths of his hazel eyes and the sensuality of his full, plump lips. They could have belonged to any one of the thousands of cupids that adorned churches throughout Venice, she mused dreamily.

* * *

Did you enjoy reading this excerpt?
Available now in audio, paperback and eBook

https://www.molliemathews.com/love-in-venice/

THANK YOU

Thank you for reading *LOVE IN GREECE*... I hope you loved it. If you did...

1. Help other people find this book by writing a review
2. Signup for my new releases email to find out about the next book as soon as I release it, sign up here http://eepurl.com/ghM501
3. Email me at mollie@molliemathews.com with a copy of your honest review and let me know if you'd love to join my dream team of advance readers
4. Follow me on BookBub: https://www.bookbub.com/authors/mollie-mathews
5. Stay in touch on Facebook: https://www.facebook.com/molliemathewsnz
6. Be inspired on Pinterest: https://nz.pinterest.com/molliemathews
7. Have fun with me on Instagram: https://www.instagram.com/molliemathewsauthor

8. Enjoy book trailers and excerpts from my books on YouTube. Be sure to subscribe! MolliemathewsYouTube

9. Follow me on TikTok: www.tiktok.com/@ mollliewritesromance

WOULD YOU LIKE TO JOIN MOLLIE'S ARC TEAM? Email me to join our exclusive group of fans and receive FREE books in exchange for your honest review—email Mollie@molliemathews.com

WOULD YOU LIKE TO JOIN MOLLIE'S READERS GROUP ON FACEBOOK? It's a private group that all of my readers are welcome to join. There is nothing that makes my heart sing than to connect with you all and talk books and writing, and I so appreciate the encouragement and support you give me.

Join Mollie's Readers Group here:
https://www.facebook.com/groups/323525616931811

ABOUT THE AUTHOR

MOLLIE MATHEWS is an award-winning artist and author known for her "sensual, beautiful, empowered stories enveloped in true romance" (Amazon review) and characters who feel real.

Whether they be Italian billionaires, handsome sheikhs, maverick cowboys, empowered heroines, or everyday people, readers of Mollie's romances say she "is a beyond compelling storyteller with the gift and the power to make you experience her remarkable craft on a whole other level."

She lives in the idyllic Bay of Islands, New Zealand, on a rural property overlooking the sea. There, surrounded by nature's beauty and inspiration, she writes her love stories. She also follows the sun, dividing her time between New

Zealand and exotic locations—wherever she intends to set her next romance novel. She lives with her romantic hero, Lorenzo—tall, dark, terribly handsome, and fluent in Spanish!

Mollie passionately believes books are medicine and the power of romance to transform people's lives. Her stories are unashamedly positive, hopeful, and optimistic. Despite the struggles and obstacles the people in her stories face, they are always rewarded with love and the happily ever after of their dreams.

Happy reading xxx

BY MOLLIE MATHEWS

THE SHEIKHS UNTAMED BRIDES

CLAIMED BY THE SHEIKH
STOLEN BY THE SHEIKH
BOUGHT BY THE SHEIKH
THE SHEIKHS UNTAMED BRIDES BOX SET BOOKS 1-2
THE SHEIKHS UNTAMED BRIDES BOX SET BOOKS 1-3

GEMSTONE BILLIONAIRES

THE ITALIAN BILLIONAIRE'S CHRISTMAS BRIDE
THE ITALIAN BILLIONAIRE'S SCANDALOUS MARRIAGE
GEMSTONE BILLIONAIRES 2 BOOK-BUNDLE BOX SET
GEMSTONE BILLIONAIRES 3 BOOK-BUNDLE BOX SET

TRUE LOVE

LOVE IN VENICE (3rd place winner Koru Award)
LOVE IN MEXICO
LOVE IN SICILY
LOVE IN MONTANA
LOVE IN TUSCANY
LOVE IN GREECE

NASHVILLE HEARTS

ONE STEP AT A TIME
LOVE RISING

PASSION DOWN UNDER SASSY SHORT STORIES

TWIST OF FATE
LOVE ME FOREVER
FOREVER AND ALWAYS
LOVE ME AS I AM
THE LIGHTKEEPER'S LOVER
FINDING A HUSBAND
LOVE ALL OF ME
CRAZY FOR YOU

PASSION DOWN UNDER 2 BOOK-BUNDLE BOX SET
(Books 1 & 2)
PASSION DOWN UNDER 3 BOOK-BUNDLE BOX SET
(Books 1, 2 & 3)
PASSION DOWN UNDER 6 BOOK-BUNDLE BOX SET

SHORT, SWEET SHEIKH LOVE STORIES
DESTINY

LUCKY

BITTERSWEET LOVE STORIES
WHAT IS SOFT IS STRONG

NASHVILLE HEARTS

ONE STEP AT A TIME
LOVE RISING

FLOURISHING HEARTS
THE GIRL IN PINK SKATES

ISBN eBook: 978-1-99-105359-6

ISBN print: 978-1-99-105360-2

Published by

Blue Orchid Publishing New Zealand

Blue Orchid
PUBLISHING

Visit www.molliemathews.com to read more about all our books and to buy them. You will also find features, author interviews and news of author events, and you can sign up for e-newsletters so that you're always first to hear about our new releases.

www.ingramcontent.com/pod-product-compliance
Lightning Source LLC
Chambersburg PA
CBHW030339020726
47493CB00004B/1337